THE GREAT SNEAK-OUT

First published in India by HarperCollins *Children's Books* 2025
An imprint of HarperCollins *Publishers*

HarperCollins Publishers India, Cyber City, Building 10-A,
Gurugram, Haryana-122002, India

www.harpercollins.co.in

2 4 6 8 10 9 7 5 3 1

Text © Sanjana Kapur 2025
Illustrations © HarperCollins Publishers India 2025

P-ISBN: 978-93-6989-546-5
E-ISBN: 978-93-6989-361-4

Sanjana Kapur asserts the moral right
to be identified as the author of this work.

All rights reserved. No part of this publication may be reproduced, stored in a retrieval system, or transmitted, in any form or by any means, electronic, mechanical, photocopying, recording or otherwise, without the prior permission of the publishers.

Without limiting the exclusive rights of any author, contributor or the publisher of this publication, any unauthorized use of this publication to train generative artificial intelligence (AI) technologies is expressly prohibited. HarperCollins also exercise their rights under Article 4(3) of the Digital Single Market Directive 2019/790 and expressly reserve this publication from the text and data-mining exception.

Series design by Denise Antao
Layout and design in Quicksand 10pt/16 by Isha Nagar

Printed and bound at Thomson Press India Ltd

*

HarperCollins Publishers, Macken House, 39/40 Mayor Street Upper,
Dublin 1, D01 C9W8, Ireland

This book is produced from independently certified FSC® paper
to ensure responsible forest management.

THE GREAT SNEAK-OUT

SANJANA KAPUR

ILLUSTRATED BY
SUNAINA COELHO

To my 6-year-old sister,
whom I hid under the
table a long time ago
Sanjana

To Orhan and Agnes
Sunaina

CHAPTER 1
My Cranky Sister Can Bite

I had been excited about starting grade three for so long but there was one thing I was dreading: my younger sister.

Mum says that she is my responsibility when we are at school. If you ask me, it's too much to expect a third-grader to be that responsible. I have barely figured out the reasons behind Pluto not being a planet anymore. Not that that's an important thing to know in order to look after your younger sibling, but it just tells you that I don't know everything.

Pa dropped us off at school on the first day. Ira was starting first grade. Everyone at home had been talking

about it for weeks. Big whoop. Been there, done that. My job was simple. I had to drop Ira to her class.

The grades in Kendra Vidya No. 2 make no sense. (We were number one in ranking and only number two in name, as our principal, Neela Sinha, liked telling us again and again.) All four sections of grades one and two are near the front. As soon as you enter the gate, to the right there's a big open area and four pale yellow blocks. Grade one and two always get more outside time so it makes sense to have a little area right outside their rooms. Further ahead are the seventh and eighth grade classrooms. These buildings are pale blue. Pale was the general colour scheme the school was going with. Be only a little excited to be here, not very excited—that's what the colours say. We third graders have to walk all the way to the other side, near the big sports field, because we are stuck in a corner. Section B, which I belong to, is at the very end. We have to cross the ninth and tenth grades and they are a very grumpy lot.

Back to Ira. I walked her to her class, like a kind and caring sister. She stood frozen at the door, holding my hand.

'Go on. I will see you when school is over.' I gently pushed her in.

'No! You also come with me,' she said, holding on tight.

Ha ha! The thought of sitting in first grade again . . . no, thank you! 'That is impossible. Now go on.'

I am not proud of what followed. Ira held my hand tighter and began crying. Big tears rolled down her cheeks and she turned a shade of bright red. I was horrified because the seventh graders were looking at us and frowning. I looked inside the dimly lit classroom and waved frantically at the teacher. Under non-school circumstances, I would have never left my sister with someone who looked like Ampoorna Ma'am. Since she had taught me two years ago, Ampoorna Ma'am had grown three new moles and her hair had changed to a bright orange-brown. She always wore the brightest colours, which didn't add up because her mood was always dark. She stomped out of the room, grouchier for having to leave forty students for one crying child.

'Your sister, Ana?' she asked, in her dragon voice.

'Yes, Ma'am.' I then shook my hand vigorously until Ira lost her grip. Ira yelled and cried, and I ran as fast as I could towards the stream of third graders. Like I said, I am not proud.

I found my best friends waiting for me. They had caught the entire Ira meltdown. Reena and Kunal had been my friends from the first day of grade one.

'What was that about?' Reena asked.

'That was just Ira being Ira. It seems school is too much for her brain,' I said.

'Poor Ira. She looked quite sad,' Kunal said.

'Oh Kunal, isn't it enough that I have to lug her to school every day?' I frowned. Kunal had a way of feeling bad for everything that made the rest of us feel bad for not feeling bad enough. Like the time a pigeon flew straight into the glass window of the staff room. He was all 'oh poor pigeon', which was true, but it was also so funny!

The rest of the day was mostly all right, except for some er . . . interesting incidents. We had to meet all of our new teachers. I am going to have to keep an eye on the maths teacher. He seemed a bit calculating, with his narrow eyes and tight lips. The Hindi teacher was too quiet for our class. All forty-seven of us had to stay extremely silent in order to hear what she was saying. Either she was too nervous or

an absolute genius because we ended up being the most well behaved in her class. I am saving my comments on the remaining for later—so far, they seem all right. I can't really hold anything against them seeing as how some of them had to teach us *and* the higher grades. The school ran on little money and big classes.

I made my way back to grade one at the end of the day. Ira was STILL crying. Some of the other kids were looking nervously at her. They trickled out slowly from the classroom, some battling with their bags, trying to straighten their straps. I hoped Ira had stopped crying at some point and just started again after a break. Ampoorna Ma'am had a strong hold on her wrist. 'Come on, Ira,' I called. 'Pa will be waiting.'

Ira squirmed in Ampoorna Ma'am's hand. 'No, Ira, what did

I say?' she said. 'Only when I say. Now stop moving. No crying, only go when I leave you. Ira, stop!'

Ampoorna Ma'am looked determined to prove she was in charge. Uh-oh. Bad idea. I started to say something, but it was too late. Ira stopped crying and gritted her teeth. Then, the same teeth sunk into the hand that was stopping her from leaving.

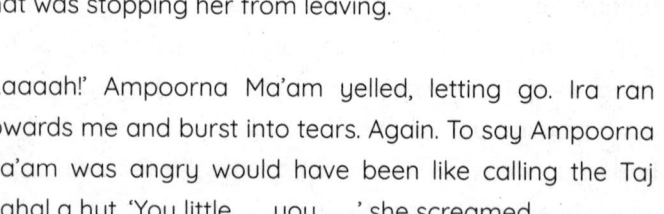

'Aaaaah!' Ampoorna Ma'am yelled, letting go. Ira ran towards me and burst into tears. Again. To say Ampoorna Ma'am was angry would have been like calling the Taj Mahal a hut. 'You little . . . you . . . ' she screamed.

I said sorry many times and repeated my successful morning tactic of running away, dragging my crybaby sister out of school. The rest was future Ana's problem.

CHAPTER 2
I Commit a School Crime

I had no idea that I would become a criminal when I woke up the next day. Happily unaware of what was going to happen, I enjoyed my morning milkshake and wolfed down my paratha. The day started out normal—or whatever we call normal. Ira yelled. Pa left us at the gate. Ira kicked and screamed. I walked her to class. We arrived at grade one to find Ampoorna Ma'am glaring at us. She had a large, white bandage around her hand, which I thought was a bit dramatic—how hard could Ira have bitten her? She ignored us and continued herding the other children in. Ira's grip became tighter.

'Ow! Ira!' I decided it was time to level with my sister. I couldn't continue to do this drama every day. So far, third grade had been dramatic enough. The English teacher, Kamala Shirin, for example, announced everyone's name loudly, like she was at a train station. Not just that, she insisted on saying them in 'English'—just to tell everyone, in case they didn't know, that she was indeed our English teacher. Some of our names weren't meant to be pronounced like that. It had taken Kunal three announcements to understand that 'Que Nail, QUE NAIL, Que Nail?' was meant to be him. Poor Que! Reena and I had decided we wouldn't let him forget his true name. Between that and the fact that in two days we were going to have our first sports period, I didn't have time for a cranky sister.

'Look, Ira. I am not far. We are in the same school. Your class is here and mine is two blocks in that direction. Just look there and you'll know I am there. You aren't alone. Just go in. I will even come and meet you during lunch break.' I hoped my brilliant motivational speech would change Ira's sobs into a hop-and-skip into her class. All it did was turn her into a slumped small sister, who turned and walked in, sobbing. I took that as a win and jolted to my class.

Reena and Que had changed our location within the class.

Yesterday, we'd sat on the third bench in the first row. Today we were in the third row, on the fifth bench. I had to agree that it was a vast improvement from yesterday's seat. I shuffled between the desk and bench, breaking Reena and Kunal's whispers.

'Why have we shifted?' I asked.

'This is much less in the teacher's face. And very nicely next to the wall, and also not right at the back. It is a sweet spot. I came in early to grab the seat.' Reena looked mighty proud of her explanation. This had clearly been her idea. 'Plus it's easy for Que to eat his lunch early in the morning.' I laughed at Kunal as his face emerged from under the desk with a bit of Maggi falling out of his mouth.

'The Maggi gets all clumpy. It is mmm mmm delicious right now. Also, stop calling me Que!' Kunal said, ducking back.

'Never!' Reena and I chimed.

Mandal Sir walked in, and we stopped mid-laugh. There are some teachers you can laugh in front of, and some in front of whom you can exchange a quick look with your friends, and then there's Mandal Sir. He's short, bald and grim. It does not matter what the weather is, he always wears brown pants, a dull shirt and a sleeveless jacket. We had reached the conclusion that he had a cupboard full of brown pants.

Reena smacked Kunal's hand just in time. He immediately put his tiffin away and stood up with the rest of us as we all droned, 'Goooood Morrrrniiiing Sirrrr...' Mandal Sir grunted a 'hmm' in return and sat down. The class sat down, too, straighter than before. Mandal Sir started flipping through the book in front of him and we all started shuffling around in our bags for our EVS books.

The class continued and I, very smartly, covered up three yawns. We were reading about how the continents had once been one large lump, when Mandal Sir got called out of the room for some admin work. I think teachers use the word admin as a way of taking a break from us. What even is admin and why does it need to get done during class? Secretly, though, I loved admin, because it meant we could waste time.

'Read the next paragraph,' Mandal Sir barked, as he left the room.

I had no intention of reading the next paragraph, so I leaned out of the window to catch a glimpse of the basketball court instead. Class nine was practising, and none of them seemed to know that the ball was meant to go into the basket.

'Ana!'

I looked at Reena, who was next to me. 'What?'

'What?' Reena said, looking up from her book.

'Why did you call me?'

'I didn't.'

'ANA!' The voice was coming from *outside* the window. I turned and Ira's face popped up.

'What are you doing here?' I had meant to whisper but you try whispering when your sister flees her class. Kunal and Reena looked up. Thankfully, no one else had heard me.

'I don't like my class.' Ira was holding her bag tightly.

'You have to go back, Ira!'

'NO!'

The no was too loud. A couple of my classmates were beginning to look up from their paragraph reading.

'Mandal Sir is coming back,' Reena whispered. 'Do something!'

'What!'

Never make decisions in a panicked state. I can say from experience that it leads you down a very twisted path. The combination of Ira's loud 'no' and Reena's hoarse whispers, Mandal Sir's footsteps and my classmates looking at me was what led to me grabbing Ira by her arms and lifting her up. Ira, immediately realizing what was happening, climbed up on a fallen brick. I slid her and her bag under our desk. My class watched in horror as the escaped first-grader vanished under the table. I'm sure hiding another student under my table is against several rules.

'Stay quiet and don't move!' I whispered, just as Mandal Sir walked in.

'Have you all finished the paragraph?'

CHAPTER 3
I Have to Deal with Farts and a Full Bladder

Ira stayed quiet for the remainder of Mandal Sir's class. Reena and Kunal stretched their legs out to hide Ira from view and the rest of the class said nothing. It was like a quiet understanding had passed through all the glances, and the entire third grade had decided to make it to the end of the class without being discovered. I had never liked my classmates more, even Frowning Asha and Farty Manav.

The next class was Kamala Ma'am's. We had a window of five-ish minutes before she arrived with a 'goood mawning styoodents'. We had to use that window to put Ira back in her class.

Farty Manav always sat next to the door, right in front. He

and Reena looked out of the door at the teachers moving between classes. 'Let's go!' Reena said.

'This is giving me a stomach ache,' Farty said, glumly. 'I don't like sneaky things. They build gas inside me.'

I coaxed Ira out of hiding. She emerged like a hero, grinning at all of my classmates as if she had been rescued from prison. To her credit, some of my classmates smiled and laughed. Some even ruffled her hair, which only encouraged the show-off to strut more.

'Come on, Ira. We have to get you back to class,' I said, trying to move her along.

'I don't want to go back!' Ira said.

Kunal, for reasons only Kunal knows, looked more unhappy than Ira. 'She doesn't want to go,' he said.

'Kunal! This isn't helping,' I said. I turned back to Ira. 'There are only two more classes before lunch. I promise I will come and see you then,' I said, ushering her through the line of my classmates towards the door.

'I'll come with you,' Kunal said, taking Ira's bag from her. He *had* to help in some way. We were just about to exit the door, when someone from the other side of the room yelled, 'ABORT ABORT!'

I turned around to see Sohail up on the desk near the window. He had propped himself up with his arms and was looking out. 'Kamala Ma'am is here! Retreat!'

Someone immediately grabbed Ira's bag from Kunal. Someone else began moving us back. Before I knew it, a triumphant Ira had been tucked back under the table. Kiran, who was seated behind us, handed Ira a banana. Ira settled down under the desk, looking relieved. Kunal had climbed up on the desks and jumped over them to reach back. I rolled my eyes. This was all unnecessary, if you asked me. Reena and I groaned and made our way back. Ira would have to stay hidden for one more class.

'Everyone, take your positions. I have lost sight of the target,' Sohail said, still aloft his perch. Again, I thought the spy talk was highly unnecessary. But it got everyone moving, so what did I know?

Everyone shuffled around, trying to settle down before Kamala Ma'am arrived. Manav, caught up in all the excitement, remained standing. He clutched the side of his stomach and looked painfully around the class. Sohail slid back into his chair just as Kamala Ma'am entered. The last-minute slide and commotion had started a giggle fit. My suspicion was that it had originated with Divya and Umaid

in the first row.

Now, normal laughter is one thing, but a giggle fit is a whole different beast. If you have ever had one, you know exactly what I mean. And if you haven't, well, then I feel both happy and sorry for you. You need to experience it to know how you can hate and love something at the same time. A giggle fit in the right environment can be wonderful. Unfortunately, this wasn't the right anything. Very soon, it had the entire class shaking. Kamala Ma'am caught on and stopped mid-attendance to look at everyone. The giggle wave died down.

'What is the matter with you lot today?' she said in a lofty voice, each word enunciated for our listening pleasure. No one answered. 'Something is certainly up. Someone explain this to me instantaneously.'

She could have said 'this instant', or 'right now'. I sometimes suspected some of her words were made up. Why would we need the word instantaneously anyway? Kamala Ma'am moved around the room and stopped at Manav. 'You, explain the joke to me.'

Poor Manav could not contain the sneakiness any longer. He stood up, looking miserable. The giggles started up again. 'Nothing, Ma'am. No joke here.' The act of lying made Manav double up in pain. He held his sides and let out a loud fart. 'Sorry! Gas.'

The laughter became louder as Manav sweated through a second fart. Kamala Ma'am scrunched up her nose and took a step back. 'My word, Manav. What *did* you have for breakfast?' She held her hand to her chest.

I felt terrible for Manav. He could have told her the truth. I was wondering what to do when I felt a tug from under the table. I glanced down and immediately knew the look on Ira's face. 'Not. Now,' I whispered. Reena looked at me.

'Please. Urgent.' Ira had crossed her legs and was clearly holding her pee in. She held the half-eaten banana up as an offering. Reena tore a bit of paper from her notebook and scribbled something on it. She nudged Kunal and passed it to him. Kunal nodded and sent it further. Reena nodded to me. To be honest, the nods were confusing, so I didn't nod back until Reena spoke. 'Take Manav to the nurse!' Immediately understanding, I got up.

'Ma'am, why don't I take Manav to the nurse? She could help him with his stomach.'

As Kamala Ma'am turned her attention to me, Ira was being ushered out from under the table. The class slowly moved her along the floor from desk to desk. I walked towards Kamala Ma'am, holding her attention on me.

'Good idea, Ana. Manav. Come on, go with Ana.'

I whispered a quick thank you to Manav, who was inching to the door. Ira had by then slunk out of the back door with the help of my class. Manav and I met her outside. She was standing cross-legged, ready to burst. The three of us hurried away as we heard Kamala Ma'am loudly say, 'QUE NAIL!'

I made a mental note never to call Manav Farty again.

CHAPTER 4
I am the Leader of a Gang

It had been two days since Ira's runaway incident. If I was being honest, I'd thought that Ira would have blabbed to Mum and Pa by now. Instead, Ira turned out to be a very talented liar. At breakfast, she would coo about how she felt like a big girl. Mum and Pa never asked for specifics, so Ira looked smug, while I frowned very hard at her. Unfortunately, the 'big girl' had made a habit of residing under my table. I'd leave her in first grade, only to find her outside the third grade classroom window looking very sad. I would try my best to coax her to go back, only to end up hiding her under the desk.

I left her again today, under the unaware glare of Ampoorna Ma'am. But the fact that Ira hadn't protested at all made me believe that she was already plotting an escape.

I found Manav standing near the door of the third grade classroom. 'Where is Ira?'

'In her class, where she should be.'

Much to my annoyance, my classmates had become increasingly involved in the whole Ira situation. Sohail had brought a small game for Ira—the kind that had water in it, with buttons to make bubbles and get tiny hoops around tiny poles. His reason: it could get boring sitting under a table with nothing but legs to look at. Ira was so happy to have entertainment that I couldn't really say much.

Vishi and Meera had brought extra fruit and a box of crayons. Reena had brought a long string, which she had looped and taught Ira some tricks with.

Between classes, someone would take up guard duty at the window and the doors. For those five minutes, my class would work like a well-oiled machine. Ira would emerge in a happy haze to be met with smiling third graders. Someone would look at her artwork, someone would give her water and she would stretch her legs. The guards would then announce the arrival of the next teacher, and everyone would take their positions. Ira being my sister had automatically made me the decider of things. I didn't feel it, but I think I was in charge. My classmates had begun asking for my opinions and often smiled at me for no reason. I still

couldn't understand why everyone was so 'one team, one dream' about this!

Manav looked disappointed with my answer. 'She'll find her way here soon, don't you think?'

'The goal is that she stays in her class. We are all going to get into trouble if we continue to hide her.' I walked into the classroom to find Reena and Kunal huddled near the desk with a couple of my other classmates.

Manav followed me in. 'But she is so miserable. I don't know how you can be so heartless.'

My classmates were getting too emotional about this. I reached the group of huddled heads. 'Ana, great! You are here. We have something of an issue,' Reena said. Kunal picked up his notepad and nodded. If I had been made the default leader of this kid smuggling gang, then Reena and Kunal had slipped into a second-in-command role. Unlike me, they were really enjoying it. I moved to the desk and placed my bag down.

'What's the problem?' I asked.

'We have sports class today. Which means that Ira might be stuck alone in here. We don't think that's a good idea. Sports Ma'am always locks the room up and we think that would cause panic.' Reena looked grim.

I looked at all their concerned faces. Asha was frowning as usual, but even in her frown there was worry. Gosh! When had Ira become the class pet?

Kunal put his notebook down on the table for everyone to see. 'Look here. We are likely to be taken to the field. This is the first sports period of third grade so I doubt anything major will be done.' He pointed at the notebook. 'This is the field. Sohail and I did some research and there are some bushes here and here. If we can figure out a way to get Ira out of the class, then we can stash her there and retrieve her later.'

'No way! That won't work.' I was not going to stuff Ira in a bush. Knowing her, she would find a butterfly, forget about staying put and just wander into the middle of us attempting to understand kho-kho. 'I know my sister and there is no way the outside will contain her. Ira will just have to stay put. And it may not even come to that. She isn't here. She may just stay in her class the entire day.'

I could see that it was not the answer my classmates wanted. 'Okay. We'll do as you say,' Reena said. 'You're the boss. You know your sister best.'

Someone at the door announced the arrival of the Hindi teacher and everyone shuffled back to their seats. Kunal stuffed his notepad into his bag grumpily. I looked out of the window and thought about the burden of being the boss of this unlikely gang.

CHAPTER 5
We Get Away with It. Almost.

Ira, like clockwork, arrived at the window during the second period. She looked like she had been crying. She didn't pop her head up or try to get my attention. I only noticed her because of her loud snotty sniffling outside the window. Sohail and Karan looked back at the sound eagerly. Kamala Ma'am was reading a story about an elephant who went out of his way to help some animals, who had been mean to him earlier. If you ask me, the elephant should have left the monkeys to get drenched in the rain. I looked out and found Ira looking straight up at me. I nodded at my classmates. Ira looked so sad today that, in that moment, I knew keeping her safe under the table had always been the right decision.

I took a piece of paper and wrote on it: 'Ira looks sad.' The paper got passed around the class and the third graders all became worried. When Karan got hold of the paper, he turned it around and wrote: 'Smuggling Operation?' He passed the paper back to me and the note made it around the room again.

Whether it was the fact that we had made it to day three of keeping a full person hidden in the class or that Ira had learnt the word 'covert' from Kunal, the stealthy notes and the spy-like behaviour of my classmates were catching up to me. It didn't feel like it was just me trying to keep my sister safe; it was a mission all of us simply had to accomplish. I tapped my nose at Karan, who nodded with half a smile. Reena grinned and Kunal's face quickly took on a very serious expression.

'AAAHA!' Karan yelled.

'What! What!' Kamala Ma'am looked up from her book, mid-word, and pulled her spectacles down. She had no idea of the spectacle that awaited her.

Karan was yelling at Ritu, who sat all the way across the room. 'YOU! I won't let you get away with it!' He stood up and slammed his hand on the table to make his made-up point.

Ritu gave an exaggerated gasp and stood up on the desk.

'You talking to me?' I couldn't help but smile. She was a natural. She waved her hands and tossed her ponytail back.

'That is right! You pencil thief!' Karan had climbed over the next desk and was hopping over the desks to get to Ritu now.

Kamala Ma'am looked astounded at the drama. She got up with a loud 'Oh my!' and strode towards Ritu and Karan. 'Get off the benches this very instant!'

This was my chance. I quickly hoisted Ira into the class and pushed her under the table. I nodded at Kunal and he stood up, a bright yellow pencil in hand. 'Oh, Karan! Your pencil had fallen down. Here it is.'

The entire class and Kamala Ma'am turned to Kunal. 'There! Que Nail has found the pencil. Please descend from those high perches.'

Karan and Ritu grinned and hopped off. 'Thank you, Quenail!' Karan said, returning to his seat. Kamala Ma'am looked a bit shaken. It was all too much for her. She instructed us to finish reading the chapter and sat, silently taking small sips from her tall metal bottle.

It had been a smooth operation. Or so it seemed. What I hadn't realized was that when Ira was being hoisted into the class, two seventh graders had been on their way to the staffroom. Five minutes after Ira was settled and Kamala Ma'am had collapsed, a note fell through the window onto my table. I looked out to see two seventh grade boys smirking evilly at me. I opened the crumpled paper and knew our little operation had run into trouble. I passed the note to Reena and Kunal.

We know your secret. Meet us at lunch by the neem tree.

CHAPTER 6
The Principal Interrupts My Dream

Sports class arrived. Ira had been given a nest in the corner of the classroom right at the back where Meera and Asha sat. Asha had left her jacket on the floor so Ira would be comfortable. After making sure she didn't have any bladder emptying needs, we left. We'd decided to take it in turns to check on her.

We all formed a line and followed Pushpa Ma'am to the ground.

'It is just thirty minutes. She'll be fine. What could go wrong?' I whispered to Reena.

'PHOO PHOO!' Reena flapped her arms. 'Don't jinx it!'

'What?'

'I don't know. My mum does it! Warding off bad luck. Why did you have to say it out loud?'

'Oh, I didn't know what I was doing!'

On the field, we were all made to line up. Pushpa Ma'am stood in front of us with her hands on her hips. She was the only teacher who could wear whatever she wanted. The other teachers were always in 'formal' clothes, as if they had an event to go to later. Pushpa Ma'am, on the other hand, was always in track pants and a loose T-shirt. Maybe that was why she was so cheerful. Her face was tiny and she had a very full head of hair to make up for it, which she kept tied into a neat but bouncy bundle.

If it wasn't for the sun, and the fact that I had a little sister alone in my classroom, I would have happily spent an hour with Pushpa Ma'am. She was going to put us into groups for our chosen sports and I was hoping to get into the football group.

She blew her whistle and we all followed her warm-up exercises. The jumping and sliding and bumping into each other almost made me forget the impending doom of the seventh graders.

After the exercises, we all tried out different things with a ball—throwing it, kicking it and pretending it was a head. We also all ran in different ways. I know what you're thinking: how many ways are there to run? You'd be surprised. Pushpa Ma'am was very smart and soon held her clipboard up to tell us our groups.

'Kho kho—Reena, Asha, Sohail, Jeevan, Sheena, Amar and Ahana.

Football—Karan, Ritu, Kunal, Ana, Manav, Abhila—'

'Ma'am Ma'am Ma'am . . . ' A student from another class had come running up to the field. She looked like she was only a year or two older to us.

'Yes yes yes?' Pushpa Ma'am replied, looking very proud of how funny she had just been.

'I have been sent to get Ana Raheja. Principal Neela wants to see her,' the student panted.

'Hmm . . . Ana please go with Vishakha to the principal's office.'

I looked around and my alarm was reflected on my classmates' faces. You did not get called to the principal's office just like that. Normally, I would act innocent until I knew what the problem was. But we all knew that I was carrying guilt the size of a first grader.

'Come on, Ana, move it. I have to announce the groups for kabaddi and throwball as well.' Pushpa Ma'am waved her clipboard at me.

I started walking, when suddenly Manav spoke. 'Ma'am I would like to go to the toilet.'

'Me too, Ma'am,' Kunal added, crossing his legs.

'Go, go. But please come back soon.'

They nodded at me, and I returned the nod. Then, I walked towards the principal's office. A lot of thoughts raced through my head. Had the seventh graders decided to rat us out before meeting us at the neem tree? Had Ampoorna Ma'am finally caught on to the fact that a student was missing? Was this the end of the third grade's secret mission? Vishakha left me at the door and I knocked.

Inside, I was met with a lot more faces than I expected. Ampoorna Ma'am was there, glaring at me; Principal Neela looked sternly from behind her neat desk; and, on the chairs in front of her desk, sat my mum and dad. Mum looked worried and Pa looked like he had a headache.

'Mum? Pa? What's wrong?' I stammered.

'Please take a seat, Ana,' Principal Neela said.

I took a seat. I was going to have to buy some time for Manav and Kunal to do whatever the head nod had meant. I had to assume it meant getting Ira out of our class and back to her own. The adults all looked grimly at me.

'Your sister, Ira, is missing from class.' Principal Neela, as usual, got straight to the point. I wish she was more of a storyteller. We needed the time.

'What do you mean? I left her in class in the morning. You saw her, Ampoorna Ma'am.' I looked around at my former teacher.

'I don't know that. A lot of children come in the morning.' Ampoorna Ma'am had clearly decided to act like she didn't know anything. I realized that if Ira was actually missing, it would be her fault. She was responsible for the first graders and an entire child had been missing from her class.

'What do you mean, Ma'am? I left her with you. She must be in her class. I just saw her.' I know this was a lofty claim, but I was confident. Well, about 72 per cent confident.

Principal Neela looked at Ampoorna Ma'am and frowned. 'Let us go and see then, shall we?' She got up and gestured for all of us to follow her. Mum placed her hand on my back and we all walked toward the grade one classroom.

CHAPTER 7
We Are Now Food Smugglers

As Mum, Pa and I followed, I asked Mum, 'Who called you to school?'

'Your principal. I don't understand, though. If Ira is in her class, where did all the fuss begin?'

'Who knows?' I shrugged. 'I was in the middle of sports class.'

'Oh! Did you get into the football group?'

'I DID! But then I was called away. I have to wait a whole week to find out about training.'

We arrived at 1A. Dread began to settle in the pit of my stomach. What if I had completely misunderstood the head nod? What if Ira wasn't back in her class? We walked towards the door. There was a substitute teacher inside, who immediately stood up.

'Ira Raheja?' Principal Neela called out.

There was no answer. Ampoorna Ma'am raised her eyebrows and looked around with a smug expression. The substitute looked around as well. Principal Neela called again. That's when I spotted the top of my sister's head. At the far end of the classroom was a small fountain of hair moving under the fan. Her head was bent low but I could recognize the way Pa tied our red ribbons anywhere. Kunal and Manav had done a good job!

'There she is,' I said. 'IRA!'

Ira lifted her head when she heard me. Her face broke into a grin. Ampoorna Ma'am's face shrivelled up into a large rotten tomato. It was like she *wanted* a kid from her class to be missing! This was as much good news for her as it was for us. Then I realized why she looked like that. Adults, especially teachers, do not like being wrong.

Ira noticed Mum and Pa and immediately ran up to them. It was clear that they would have to take her home.

'Well, well.' Principal Neela looked at Ampoorna Ma'am and my parents.

'This has been a huge waste of time,' my father announced, picking Ira up. 'If it is okay with you, we would like to take Ira back home with us.'

'Of course! We are so sorry. It's just that we have to follow through on missing reports. And our teachers had done a thorough check. I don't know how we missed her,' Principal Neela said. She shot a glance at Ampoorna Ma'am. It was not a good glance.

After many huffs and glares and apologies, the adults dispersed, with a very happy Ira. It was almost lunch time. I made my way back to my class. Most of my classmates had returned by the time I got there. The all looked at me, waiting for me to fill them in.

'It was fine. Ira was there and Ampoorna Ma'am looked mad. But, for the time being, the situation is contained,' I reported. 'Kunal and Manav, you were great!'

They both beamed. I smiled back and continued, 'We have a new problem, though. A couple of seventh graders saw me smuggling Ira into the classroom. Reena, do you have the note?'

Reena produced it and everyone crowded around to read it. 'We need to figure out what they want. They haven't ratted us out yet, so there must be something they want,' Reena said.

I looked at my classmates. None of them had signed up for this, yet they all looked equally worried.

'I would like to come with you,' Kunal said.

'So would I,' Sohail added.

'I want to come with you too,' Ritu said from behind, and Reena added a 'me too'.

I had close to ten volunteers and counting in a matter of a minute.

'If you don't mind my stomach grumblings, I would also like to come. A stronger force would make all the difference,' Manav said.

I laughed and Kunal put his arm around a very nervous Manav. 'You've done enough for today, Manav.'

'I think five should be enough. There are just two of them. We'll meet them and report back here.'

The bell for the lunch break went off and Kunal, Reena, Sohail, Ritu and I marched towards the big tree in the middle of the school. It was usually crowded at lunch time. I imagined us walking in slow motion. If it wasn't for the two older kids that we were going to face, it would have been a lot cooler.

The two boys were at the tree when we arrived. They looked a bit alarmed to see so many of us but quickly got over it. One of them was tall, with hair flopping down on his forehead. The other one was shorter with a sneer stuck to his face. The shorter one had large hands, which were hard to miss because he constantly rubbed them together like an overgrown fly. The taller one spoke.

'Aha, the sneaky kids are here,' he said, laughing at his non-joke. 'Who was that kid you helped climb into your class?'

'What do you want?' I asked, ignoring his question. The fact that I wasn't alone made me speak with more confidence than I felt inside. Big kids scared me. They behaved all adult-like in front of people smaller than them. Pretend adults were scarier than the real ones.

'What can you give us in exchange for keeping your secret?' the big boy said, his sneery friend nodding along.

'What do you like?' I asked.

'Chips, samosas . . .' he began.

'Ooh . . . laddoos! Oh, and-and those pakoras we get at the canteen,' Big Hands added.

I looked around at my friends. Reena was rolling her eyes so much I feared they would fall off her head. The rest of them were trying their best to look a combination of tough and grim, but I could see my panic being reflected on their faces. I turned back to the two boys. 'We don't have any of that. Can't you just not tell anyone about what you saw?'

'Ha ha! That isn't how this will work. Third graders get an extra snack break. That means you must have something. We will be here every lunch break. We better get something in exchange for our silence,' said the tall one.

Kunal stepped up beside me. 'We'll figure something out. Just keep your mouths shut.'

'Much better. See you tomorrow!' The boys ruffled Kunal's hair, not in a 'you are so sweet' way but in a 'we know where to find this head' way.

We walked back to class to figure how we would smuggle food to our new clients.

CHAPTER 8
The Third Grade Mafia Gets Too Big for its Shoes

When you have forty-six classmates, and all of them act like one team, there comes a time when you believe you can do anything.

After our chat with the two worst boys in Class 7, everyone pitched ideas and soon we had something we could put into action. Some of the suggestions were just plain bad and were shut down immediately. We weren't going to steal, we were sure of that. We agreed on one thing, though. We were going to have to lie. Everyone went home that day with a plan.

We were all going to request our parents for more food. We were also going to complain about how little they fed us.

No parent can resist feeding their child more. The last and ultimate weapon we had up our sleeves was comparison. Besides making demands for what we 'felt' like eating, we would tell our parents how 'Asha had brought the tastiest samosa', and how 'the bread pakoras by Sohail's dadi were fantastic'.

Well, the plan worked.

Three days later, on the table in front of us were five cookies, four bread pakoras, one dabba of onion bhajjis and two pieces of cake. It wasn't a bad start.

The next two days got better. 'Let's not spoil them. If we show them how good we are at this,' Reena said, 'they'll expect a large feast each time.'

'You are right,' Asha said. She had brought an empty dabba from home, into which she put two bread pakoras, two onion bhajjis and two cookies. 'Keep the rest.'

We decided that drop offs would only be done by one of the original five who had met the Hungry Hooligans. Meanwhile, Ira had been escaping with increasing regularity. What I gathered from her was that Ampoorna Ma'am had been super annoyed about being proven wrong. So, if Ira hated her class before, she hated it even more now. She was ignored for the most part, which made it even easier for her to escape. We now had a cushion stashed under the table for her to sit on.

We also wanted to try and avoid another run-in with the principal. Instead of hiding Ira all the time, we had a special task force to smuggle her back into her class sometimes. Food, kids, we could move anything without being seen in the school.

On day seven, Kunal and I took the dabba to the neem tree. Today's delivery had two samosas, two dal vadas and three homemade biscuits. Our customers were already waiting, but with them was a tall girl. She sat behind them, reading. She looked completely disinterested in us.

'We have your dabba,' I said.

'Let's see what we have today,' Floppy Hair said. He opened the dabba and sighed with glee. 'See, Sindhuja! Didn't we tell you we had minions?' He held the dabba out to the girl. She lowered her book, looking unimpressed. She picked out a biscuit and bit into it.

'Not bad,' she said. She went back to her book. She must have taken another bite because she lowered her book and looked at her friends. 'Do you get a dabba from these,' she nodded her head towards us, 'every day?'

'Yeah yeah!' Big Hands said. 'That is the deal.'

'May we go now?' I asked, and Big Hands waved us off. The two of them tucked into the contents of the box.
As Kunal and I walked back, I turned to him. 'I don't like that girl. I don't like the idea of more people being involved.'

Kunal shrugged. 'I don't think she's going to be a problem. She looked like she was in on it, and I don't think those boys want their supply to stop.'

'I don't know, Kunal. I don't like it.'

Boy, was I right. On Monday, we all arrived and made our way to assembly. Each class stood in two straight lines, beginning with the first graders and going all the way up to twelfth grade. Most teachers were assigned to the first grade. After assembly was done, the neat lines made their way back to their classes. Of course, that's when neatness was replaced with criss-crossing, zig-zagging, traffic-jamming non-lines.

On our way back, I got what is called a 'sidey' look from the shadows. It was accompanied by the kind of sound

someone makes to call a dog or a cat on the road. When I heard the sound the first time I didn't look up because there was no way someone was calling me with a 'chsh-chsh'. But then it got louder and Ritu, who was standing behind me, nudged me.

'I think those girls are calling you,' she said.

'Me? Those girls are in eleventh grade.' Despite not believing it, I looked in their direction and pointed at myself, looking confused. They nodded vigorously, confirming that it was me they wanted. I broke away from the line and went to them. Eleventh graders did not talk to third graders. It just made no sense.

'You Ana?' one of them asked.

'Yes.'

'We heard you and your class can move anything secretly?'

'Umm ... who told you that?'

'My sister. She is in seventh grade.'

I frowned. 'Is your sister's name Sindhuja?'

'Ohh, look at you. Don't you have all the information.'

'I think you have the wrong person.' I turned to leave when Sindhuja's sister put her pointy finger on my shoulder.

'I think we have exactly the right person. Now, here's what you will be doing for us.' One of the other girls held out two notebooks, which were handed to me.

'What do you want?' I asked. Third grade students are usually so neglected in school that, until you cross fifth grade, you fly under the radar without too much happening. You aren't the youngest and you haven't become big enough to matter in inter-school sports and debate teams. So, when an eleventh grader asks for something, you don't argue.

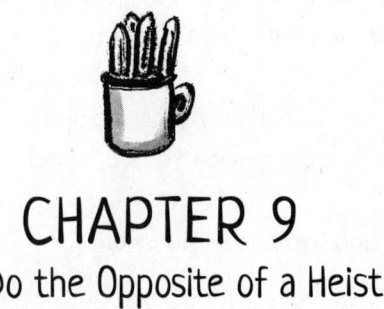

CHAPTER 9
We Do the Opposite of a Heist!

The third grade classroom was a gloomy place. We all stared at the two notebooks. If you ask me, this had all gotten out of hand too quickly. How had we gone from one sad little sister, nine days ago, to being given dangerous tasks by eleventh graders?

'Apparently they were supposed to submit this yesterday but they were late in completing their work. Mandal Sir will only realize the notebooks are missing when he checks their work because a student usually collects all the books and hands them over to him. So, they want us to sneak in and put these in the eleventh grade pile before he checks the notebooks.'

'No! Not Mandal Sir! Anyone but him,' Kunal sighed.

'I don't think I have a choice,' I said.

'You? Let's be clear. You aren't doing this on your own,' Reena said, and the others nodded.

'This isn't as simple as hiding Ira under the table. One person will be able to slip in easily,' I said.

'What are you thinking?' Ritu asked.

'I will go during one of the morning classes. Teachers don't usually have a free period in the morning so the room should be empty. I just have to figure out where Mandal Sir sits. In and out, that's the plan.' I sounded more confident than I actually was. I had never been to the staffroom before and it scared me. 'Has anyone been inside the staffroom?'

A small voice from the back of the class spoke. 'I have.'

We all turned around. Ameya was the tiniest, neatest and most quiet girl in class. She spoke so little that we often forgot she was there. Especially because she was Ritu's best friend and Ritu spoke enough for twelve people at the same time. I'd never understood that friendship. Ritu jumped with joy and climbed over a desk to sit next to her friend. She held her shoulders and shook them. 'OF COURSE!' Ameya grinned at her.

'Ameya is the one who takes all the notebooks to the staffroom for us,' Ritu said, proudly.

'She does?' I was so confused. I had never ever given it any thought. But it made sense. How else were the notebooks getting there and back? All the teachers seemed to walk around with nothing in their hands.

'Tell them, Am! You know where all the teachers sit.' Ritu smiled.

And that is when I saw why Ritu was so fond of her. Ameya the Tiny got up from her seat and walked to the centre of the group. She was instantly in charge. 'Someone give me a sheet of paper and a pen, please.' Pen and paper in hand, she began to work in a way that can only be performed by a mastermind. In swift strokes, she drew the layout of the staffroom, complete with windows, doors and cupboards. With each table she drew, she described the teacher.

'This here is Kamala Ma'am. She keeps her table neat and uses the drawers to maximum capacity. The only thing on her table is her water bottle and her notebook with one pen. Next to her is Tamanna Ma'am. Her table is as uneventful as she is.' Ameya paused to let the giggles die down and immediately dove back in. 'Ravi Sir sits at the end here. He has a lot of stuff on his table. We get it, you are the math teacher, there is no need to prove it with five protractors on one table.' Ritu laughed loudly and Ameya paused again. 'On the other side, right opposite, is Mandal Sir's table. There is a row of cupboards in between along this wall. Mandal Sir usually keeps at least three neat piles of notebooks on his table at all times. Extremely neat. So, Ana, you will have to make sure everything is exactly the way it was if you want to leave no room for suspicion. He also has a bunch of red pens in his pen stand and . . .'

'Teacher approaching. Everyone back to your seats,' Manav announced. He usually liked being the lookout.

As everyone scrambled back to their seats, Ameya held my hand, 'Good luck.'

I nodded and picked up the notebooks and Ameya's map. I took my seat just as Kamala Ma'am walked in. It was now or never. I was just about to excuse myself, when a small hand appeared on the windowsill. Ira was here too early. I nudged Reena. Kamala Ma'am was busy opening the attendance register and looking for the right page. Reena took her notebook and walked straight to her. I quickly hoisted Ira in. We had become so good at it that we barely thought about it anymore. I looked down at Ira and whispered, 'You'll have to go back today, Ira. I have to leave the class.'

Ira looked with a frown at me. 'Not now. No.'

'Ira, please.' I could see Reena was returning, so I straightened up. Reena took her seat next to me. 'Look after her,' I said.

Reena smiled and nodded. I stuffed the two notebooks under my shirt and hoped they would hold in my belt. I got up. 'Ma'am, may I be excused?'

Kamala Ma'am never asked why we wanted to be excused.

My guess was that she didn't like knowing if we needed to go number 1 or 2. 'Of course, of course,' she said, waving me out.

Once out, I hurried towards the staffroom. The school had quietened down. After the rush of assembly, it was always eerie how silent it got. We were all so well-behaved in the morning. I arrived at the staffroom and looked in through the window. Ameya had been on point. Right down to the smallest drawer, everything was exactly how she had drawn it. Only Ravi Sir was inside. He was gathering some papers and grumbling loudly to himself. I heard the words 'stupid, ugh, you fool, argh' and some other things that we weren't allowed to say out loud. He rushed out of the room a moment later.

This was my chance. It was empty. I slipped into the room and made my way straight to Mandal Sir's table. Sure enough, there were three stacks of notebooks there. The eleventh grade stack was in the centre. I carefully picked up the top three notebooks, took the two notebooks I had and placed them down.

A sudden sound from behind made me jump and I looked around. There was nothing there. I didn't have time for random sounds. I scolded myself and placed the other notebooks back. I neatened the pile and grinned. It was done! I had done it. I couldn't believe I had gotten away with

it. I turned around to leave and all the happiness left me as quickly as it had come.
'How can I help you, Miss Ana?'

I stood frozen as Mandal Sir walked towards me.

CHAPTER 10
I Don't Like Interrogations

When I first hid Ira under my desk, I always knew I would get caught some day. I hoped that I wouldn't, but there was a part of me that just knew that we would one day reach a dead end. I definitely hadn't imagined that any of it would involve me standing face-to-face with Mandal Sir. I wanted to pee, I was sweating and I was suddenly thinking about how loose my socks were. Mandal Sir's narrowed eyes and tilted head were not helping me come up with a good answer to what I was doing at his desk. What came out of my mouth was most unconvincing.

'I needed a red pen, sir.' I picked a red pen from the stand.

Mandal Sir pulled a chair from behind him, and placed it

next to his table. 'Please sit.' He pulled another chair and sat down opposite the still-empty chair. Seeing no way out, I sat.

'I know that I have a lot of red pens but I doubt *this* was the first place you thought to look. Students don't usually come into the staffroom voluntarily. So, I am going to ask you again, how can I help you?'

I blinked. Mandal Sir spoke very little. I had never seen him up close. The light from the one tube-light in the room bounced off his bald head and gave him a warm yellow glow. He even looked amused, which wasn't an expression you associated with him usually. He sat back, waiting for me to answer. I was calculating how long it had been since I had left class. No one took this long for a toilet break. Mandal Sir raised his eyebrows to remind me that I still hadn't answered. I knew that!

'Okay, I can see that you don't have an answer. Why don't you tell me this then,' Mandal Sir crossed his legs and leaned in a bit. 'How is your sister doing now? Has she adjusted to the new school or is she still hiding under your desk?'

'What?' I had stumbled through that 'what'. Because what! How did he? What?

Mandal Sir grinned. Yes, you heard me right. He was most definitely grinning. He wasn't smiling, he was grinning. He looked like a completely different person. I was so glad for that grin because, even though everything from the last week or so was tumbling around inside my head, I wasn't afraid. For the first time since this school year had started, I wasn't afraid of someone finding out the truth. Someone knew, and I was so happy that someone knew. I took a deep breath and decided I was going to talk.

'How did you know, Sir?' I asked.

'You didn't think you could hide an entire student under the table and no one would notice, did you?' Mandal Sir smiled.

'I actually did,' I said. I really did think I had gotten away with it.

'Well, *I* noticed. Now, do you want to tell me what you are doing here?'

'It is a long story and I have only excused myself for the toilet. Kamala Ma'am will be wondering where I am.'

'I will explain things to Kamala Ma'am. And I have two free periods right now, so I'm in the mood for your story.'

Seeing no way out, I told Mandal Sir everything. The more I told him, the better I felt. He asked me a few questions but he mostly just listened. No adult had ever listened to me for this long! I told him every little detail and he looked very entertained. At the end, he nodded and was quiet for a while. I wondered why I had been so afraid of him. After what seemed like forever, he got up.

'Come on, let me drop you back to class.'

I followed him and we walked in silence for a bit. I had so many questions. Why wasn't I immediately in trouble? What was Mandal Sir going to do? Instead, I asked him something else. 'Are you secretly nice?'

He smiled. 'Is it a secret? I thought I was openly nice.'

'No, you aren't. Everyone is scared of you.'

'Ah! Interesting.' He paused for a bit. 'You know that you can't keep hiding your sister, right?'

'I know.'

'Okay, good.'

Kamala Ma'am was surprised to see me return with another teacher, but there was an audible gasp from my class when they saw Mandal Sir with me. 'I am sorry for keeping your student away, Kamala. I needed a quick errand and Ana was most helpful,' Mandal Sir said, as he led me in.

Kamala Ma'am nodded. 'Of course, of course, Mr Mandal. It is no problem at all.'

Mandal Sir left without another word and I took my seat. From under the table, Ira grinned and waved at me and I couldn't help but smile.

CHAPTER 11
We Are Legendary

I got bombarded with questions as soon as Kamala Ma'am left the class. I tried my best to give short answers. But before I could say anything much, there was something else I had to do. Making sure that Manav was watching the door, I ducked under the table. Ira looked at me.

'You have to go back to your class, Ira,' I said. I held her hand.

'Why? I like it here. I like your class. Your friends are nice,' Ira said.

'Because, Ira, this is my class. You have to be in yours. You will one day be in grade three but you have to come to grade three *with* your classmates.'

'I don't like it there.'

'I know. But I promise it will get better. How do you think I made all these friends? I stayed in my class. You'll also make friends. We'll all always be right here in case you ever need anything. But you have to try.'

Ira popped her head out and looked at my class. Everyone was looking in our direction and they all waved at Ira. She grinned and waved back. 'Okay,' she finally said.

'Okay?'

'Yes,' she said. 'But can I stay here till lunch break?'

'You definitely can.'

At lunch, Reena, Kunal and I dropped Ira back to her class.

'Does everyone like their teachers?' Ira asked, looking at all three of us.

'Nope. In fact, a lot of us become friends talking about how much we don't like them,' Kunal said.

'Some are nice,' Ira said, looking at the door of her class. 'I'll try, Ana.'

After making sure Ira was okay, we went to deliver the dabba. When we reached the tree, we found Floppy Hair and Big Hands waiting. They looked at us and immediately got up. I held the dabba towards them and they took a step back. Weird. I held it up closer to them. 'Take it. It is all there,' I said. They stepped back again.

'We don't want it. Who said we wanted it? We never said it. Thank you very much!'

I frowned. Kunal and Reena were looking as confused as me. 'I am sorry. You don't want your treats anymore?'

'Anymore? We don't know what you are talking about. We didn't ask for anything. Don't ever come back here,' Big Hands said.

'Yea. Sorry about the confusion,' Floppy Hair said.

With that, they turned and left, walking really fast. So very weird.

We walked back to class with our dabba of goodies. 'That was weird, right? What do you think happened?' Kunal finally asked.

'Not sure. But I suppose we don't have to supply them with food anymore,' I said. I had a feeling that my chat with Mandal Sir had something to do with it. Back in the classroom, I told the entire class everything in great detail. When I said Mandal Sir was kind and nice, they all refused to believe it.

'What! How is that even possible?' Sohail said.

'None of this makes sense. Shouldn't we be in trouble?' Ritu was most surprised. I had a feeling she was used to being in trouble.

'We should. But we aren't. And the seventh graders have left us alone too. So, I suppose Mandal Sir is nice.'

Everyone sunk into a thoughtful silence.

'What about Ira?' Kunal asked.

'We can't keep hiding her,' I said.

'But what else can we do? She still hates her class,' Reena said.

'Then we have to help her make friends and help her love her classmates,' I said. 'As much as I love mine.' I looked around at my classmates and turned red in the face. I couldn't have asked for better friends.

The next day, I found Mandal Sir walking back to the staffroom and ran up to him.

'Hello, Sir!'

'Good morning, Ana. How can I help you?'

'I have a question.'

'Ask away.'

'Why didn't I get into trouble? In fact, the opposite happened. I must have broken a dozen rules and lied several times. Why didn't you tell anyone?'

Mandal Sir smiled. 'Because, Ana, I was once a scared

younger sibling who needed rescuing. Not many can say they formed an underground gang in their school just to keep their little sister safe.'

I grinned. 'Thank you, Sir.' I ran back to my class. The first thing I wanted to do was tell them about my conversation.

One thing I was sure of was that Ira wasn't going to feel alone in school ever again.

All discussions over, grade 3B walked out of the classroom in separate groups after what seemed an age. I knew, though, that we were truly one large gang now. We had gotten so used to huddling inside to make sure all plans were working well. So, when we walked out, we walked out to a very different Kendra Vidya No. 2.

Different versions of everything that had happened had spread through the school. The eleventh graders would nod at us when we walked by. We would randomly get fist bumps and high fives in the corridors from students much older to us. The story had spread and taken various forms but the bottom line was, we were legends.

ACKNOWLEDGEMENTS

I want to begin by thanking Tina Narang, who thought up the idea of POFFS in a bid to continue to make wonderful children's literature.

Sunaina, thank you for loving the characters so much and making them your own. Every sketch you drew made it worth writing this story.

Thank you, Denise, for the design of the entire collection; Isha for designing the book so well; and Akshay and Ankita for the eagle-eyed proofing.

Thank you, Nimmy Chacko, for the astute copy editing and for being the best title giver for all books everywhere.

Biggest and brightest thank you to Aparna Kapur for just being one of the best editors around. When you love a story you really put everything behind it and it is always inspiring to work with you.

And lastly thank you to my innermost circle of trust and comfort, Subhir, Paru and Pip.

ABOUT THE AUTHOR

Sanjana Kapur is an author and editor with over 15 years of experience in children's publishing. She has written several books for children, including the award-winning *Who Stole Bhaiya's Smile?* Sanjana has also hosted quiz shows and children's events in schools across India. She is always making futile attempts to make sense of the world.

ABOUT THE ILLUSTRATOR

Sunaina Coelho is a designer and illustrator. She was born in New Delhi, studied at the National Institute of Design, Ahmedabad, and currently lives in Bangalore with her family.